This book belongs to

Princess _____

❦ ❧ 𝒫 ❧ ❦

The Royal Disney Princess Club

Every Disney Princess Loves Nature

Nature

Story by Sara Miller. Crafts and activities by Kris Hirschmann.
Photography by White Light Incorporated, Bethel, CT
Design by Mark A. Neston Design

Published by Scholastic Inc., 90 Old Sherman Turnpike, Danbury, CT 06816.

For information regarding permission, write to: Disney Licensed Publishing, 114 Fifth Ave., New York, NY 10011.

ISBN-13: 978-0-545-08516-8 ISBN-10: 0-545-08516-0
U.K. ISBN-13: 978-0-545-08556-4 U.K. ISBN-10: 0-545-08556-X

Printed in Singapore

First printing, October 2008

Sleeping Beauty
Flowers for Aurora

A Storybook with Crafts & Activities

Early one spring day, not long after Princess Aurora and Prince Phillip were married, Phillip suggested they spend the morning in the forest. Aurora was delighted. Because even though the princess loved castle life, she often missed being surrounded by nature—the tall trees, the fragrant flowers, the sound of the babbling brook, and her wildlife friends.

"I know why the forest is so special to you," said Phillip, as he and Aurora sat in the shade of a tree. "But do you know why it's special to me?"

Aurora shook her head.

"Because it's the place I met you," he said with a twinkle
in his eye. "And to remind us both of this beautiful place,"
Phillip continued, "I want to give you this." He held out his
hand to reveal a sparkling flower pendant.

"Oh, how lovely! It looks just like a wildflower," cried
Aurora, as Phillip clasped the pendant around her neck. "I'll
wear it always. Thank you."

Phillip answered with a loving smile.

Later, at the castle,
Aurora kept thinking about
how sweet and thoughtful
Prince Phillip's gift was.

When it was time for tea with her fairy aunts—Flora, Fauna, and Merryweather—she eagerly told them about the flower pendant.

"I want to do something special for Phillip, too," Aurora said. "I was thinking of decorating the ballroom with lots of wildflowers. Then Phillip and I can dance the night away surrounded by nature."

The three good fairies all nodded, happy to help.

"I'll need a gown to wear," Aurora said thoughtfully. "Something simple yet beautiful, like my pendant."

"Oh, I have the perfect gown in mind!" cried Merryweather. And before the princess could blink, she found herself dressed in a very fancy blue ball gown. "There!" Merryweather said, pleased with herself. "Blue looks *so* lovely on you!"

"Blue is very nice," Aurora agreed.
"Yes," Flora chimed in. "But I know what
would make your gown even more special."
"What?" Aurora wondered.

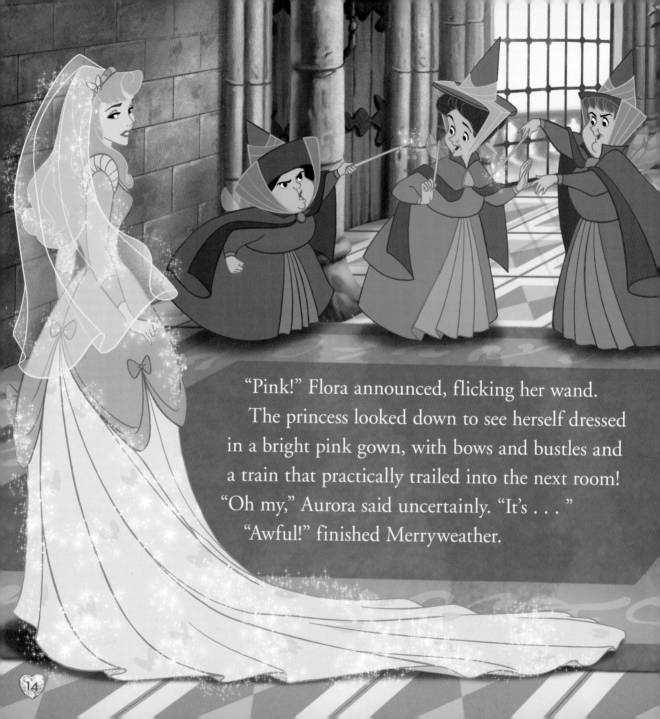

"Pink!" Flora announced, flicking her wand.
The princess looked down to see herself dressed
in a bright pink gown, with bows and bustles and
a train that practically trailed into the next room!
"Oh my," Aurora said uncertainly. "It's . . ."
"Awful!" finished Merryweather.

Merryweather and Flora
began to argue, but Fauna held
up her hands. "Now, now, girls,
you must work together on the
dress," she reminded them.

"Fine," sniffed Merryweather.
"I'll just change the hair band
and add some beads."

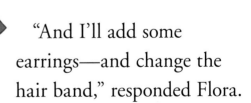

"And I'll add some
earrings—and change the
hair band," responded Flora.

The two fairies began
making one change after
another to Aurora's outfit.

"Enough!" Fauna said, interrupting the other fairies. "Let's ask Aurora what *she* thinks of the dress."

The princess looked down. Her dress was pink and blue in all the wrong spots, with so many prints and patterns swirling around that it actually made her dizzy to look at it. "Well, it certainly is—bright," she said finally, not wanting to hurt anyone's feelings. "But I need you dears to help me with one more important thing."

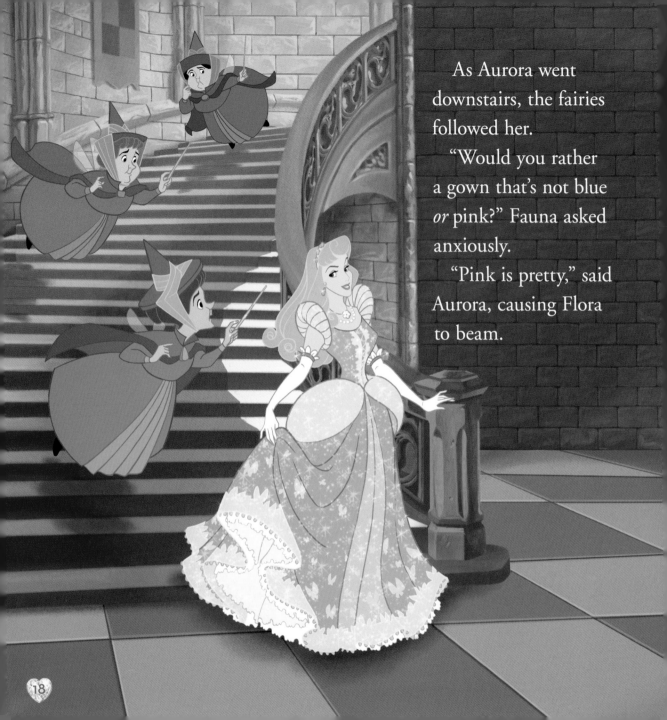

As Aurora went downstairs, the fairies followed her.

"Would you rather a gown that's not blue *or* pink?" Fauna asked anxiously.

"Pink is pretty," said Aurora, causing Flora to beam.

"And blue?" asked Merryweather.

"Blue is beautiful," Aurora answered kindly. "But I must get back to the forest to pick wildflowers to fill the ballroom. I need you three to make sure Phillip doesn't know where I am or what I'm doing so that he'll be surprised."

"Of course, dear," said Flora. "Leave it to us."

The fairies changed Aurora's dress
back to normal so that she could
return to the forest. Her woodland
friends were surprised and pleased
to see her back so soon. They
helped the princess find dozens
and dozens of fragrant wildflowers.
Soon her entire basket was full.
After promising her friends that she
would visit them again soon, Aurora
returned to the castle.

Aurora began to decorate the ballroom with the flowers she had picked. She put some of the bouquets into vases, and then she braided the stems of the rest of them to make pretty floral garlands. While she worked, she hummed a little tune to herself.

When all the flowers had been arranged, she began to hang the garlands. But Aurora soon realized she hadn't picked enough flowers to decorate the entire room. "I want it to be perfect," she thought. "I might have just enough time for one more flower-gathering trip."

Aurora rushed back to the forest and began collecting more wildflowers. She filled her basket quickly, but she still wasn't sure she would have enough. She tucked some extra blossoms in her hair as well. By now, though, the sun was setting and darkness began to fall over the forest. "Oh, dear," Aurora said with concern. "Phillip will be worried."

"Now, why would I worry?" Aurora heard a voice behind her say. It was Phillip! "The fairies were trying to keep me away from the forest, so I knew exactly where to find you," explained Phillip, laughing.

"But I had planned a surprise for us," Aurora began, disappointed. "I wanted to give you an evening as lovely as the pendant you gave to me, with flowers and dancing and . . ."

"But this evening *is* lovely," said Phillip with a smile. "The flowers in your hair are almost as beautiful as you are." Then he looked around the forest. "And I couldn't imagine a more magnificent ballroom."

"Oh, Phillip," Aurora sighed happily.

"Shall we dance?" Phillip asked, wrapping his arms around his wife.

Aurora nodded. And so, with the rustling of the tall trees for music, the royal pair danced the night away.

The End

Every Disney Princess Loves Nature

Nature

This month's princess theme is nature.

These crafts and activities will show you different ways
to appreciate the natural world around you.

Aurora's Crafts & Activities

Princess Aurora is happiest when she's spending time in
the forest surrounded by nature. Turn the page to discover
Aurora's crafts and activities about nature.

Aurora's Necklace

Aurora beams with joy when she wears the necklace from Prince Phillip. You will beam, too, whenever you wear this flowery pendant that you create yourself!

- Translucent white snap-on lid, such as one from a coffee can
- Marker or pen
- Scissors
- Glitter glue (any color)
- White glue
- Sequins (any color)
- ½-inch (1.3-mm)-long drinking straw segment
- No-longer-needed chain necklace

With a grown-up's help:

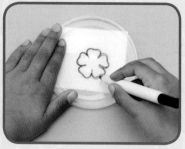

1. Trace the flower shape on this page onto white paper. Then lay the lid on top of the flower shape and trace the flower onto the lid.

2. Cut out the flower shape.

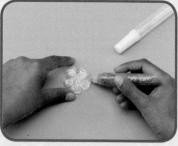

3. Decorate the flower with glitter glue. Then glue three or four sequins to the center of the flower. Set the flower aside to dry.

4. Once the glue is completely dry, turn the flower over. Glue the straw segment just above the flower's center where shown.

5. Thread one end of the necklace through the straw. Put both ends around your neck and close the clasp to wear your creation!

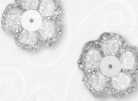

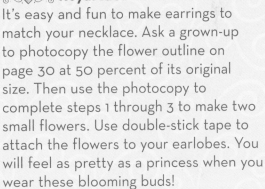
♡ Royal Idea

It's easy and fun to make earrings to match your necklace. Ask a grown-up to photocopy the flower outline on page 30 at 50 percent of its original size. Then use the photocopy to complete steps 1 through 3 to make two small flowers. Use double-stick tape to attach the flowers to your earlobes. You will feel as pretty as a princess when you wear these blooming buds!

Pretty Petals Challenge

Things don't stay the same shade for long around Aurora's fairy aunts! Help the fairies to transform the blooms in this flowery and fun game.

Number of players:

It takes three players to play this game.

Get ready:

✿ Ask a grown-up to make one copy of page 33 for each player.

✿ Gather one die and a green, blue, and pink crayon, colored pencil, or marker.

✿ Each player chooses a color. The green player will color Fauna's flower, the pink player will color Flora's flower, and the blue player will color Merryweather's flower.

How to play:

✿ Player 1 rolls the die. The player gets to color the part of his or her flower that matches the number on the die. When he or she is done, the die passes to the next player.

✿ Players take turns rolling the die and coloring their flowers.

✿ If a player rolls a number that he or she has already colored, he or she loses a turn, and the die passes to the next player.

✿ The first player to color the entire flower earns fairy wings and wins the game!

Flora

Fauna

Merryweather

Blooming Cake

This blooming cake would add the perfect touch to Aurora's flower-themed celebration—or to *your* next party!

With a grown-up's help:

1. Make two round cakes according to the directions. Remove the cakes from the pans. When the cakes are cool, push the open end of the can down through the center of one cake.

2. Carefully remove the can and the cake circle you just cut and set it aside.

3. Cut the remaining cake ring into six equal pieces as shown to make flower petals.

Crafts & Activities

4. Place the other round cake onto the serving plate. Arrange the six petals evenly around the round cake.

5. Use frosting to "glue" the flower shape together. Cover the entire flower cake with frosting.

6. Decorate your cake with decorative icing, sprinkles, colored sugar, candies, or anything else you like to make your cake fancy enough for a princess's tea party!

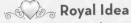 **Royal Idea**

Make a mini cake out of the small cake circle you set aside in step 2. Decorate it with any leftover frosting, sprinkles, and other tasty decorations for a delicious, fairy-sized treat!

Celebrate Nature!

Don't wait for birthdays or other big days to celebrate—recognize smaller occasions, too! Bake a Blooming Cake to make any day special. Or you might bake a batch of cupcakes and arrange them like a bouquet of flowers.

A few reasons to celebrate:

- ❀ A sunny day
- ❀ A new friendship
- ❀ A playdate
- ❀ A full moon
- ❀ The first day of spring
- ❀ A new pet

Flower Power

Princesses love to add special touches to their everyday activities. Freshen up your cards, letters, notes, and other writing tasks with this fun, flowery pencil.

What You Need

- Ruler
- Pencil or pen
- Scissors
- Large piece of tissue paper (any flowery color)
- Twist tie
- Pencil
- Piece of green tissue paper
- Glue stick
- Tape
- Glitter glue

With a grown-up's help:

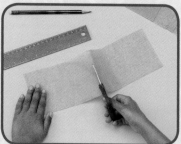

1. Measure, mark, and cut six 4- x 6-inch (10- x 15-cm) pieces of tissue paper. (**Hint:** Use an index card to trace around the edges instead of measuring.) Stack the pieces of tissue paper, making sure the edges are even.

2. Accordion-fold the stack, the short way as shown, making the folds about 3/8 inch (1 cm) wide. Bend the twist tie around the center of the folded tissue and twist the tie against the folded tissue to keep it closed.

3. Starting with the top sheet, gently pull up both sides of each sheet of tissue paper to separate them.

Crafts & Activities

4. Lay the pencil on the piece of green tissue paper. Measure, mark, and cut the tissue paper as long as the pencil's barrel and about 2 inches (5 cm) wide. Carefully smear glue over the paper.

5. Tape the ends of the twist tie to the eraser end of the pencil.

6. Place the pencil onto one long edge of the green tissue paper as shown. Carefully roll the tissue paper around the pencil, smoothing the paper as you go. Decorate the edges of your tissue paper flower with glitter glue.

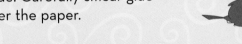 **Royal Idea**
A bouquet makes a wonderful gift for a special friend: Turn one dozen new pencils into tissue-paper flowers. Then give the bouquet to your best friend as a reminder that your friendship is *always* in bloom!

Pot Full of Flowers

A small flowerpot makes an adorable holder for your blooming pencils. Clean the pot and paint it if you wish. Once the paint dries, decorate the pot with stickers, ribbons, or anything else you like. Fill the pot with glass rocks; then poke your pencils between the rocks so that they can stand up straight and pretty!